Heathers Book

Look for more books by Heather Gilbert at www.heathersbook.com

THE MICE BEFORE CHRISTMAS

Written and Illustrated by Heather Gilbert

THEY CHEWED HOLES in THE StOCKinGS tHAt WERE HUnG UP WitH CARe anD LEFt DOZEnS OF SUGAR COOKiE CRUMBS aLL OVER tHE CHaiR.

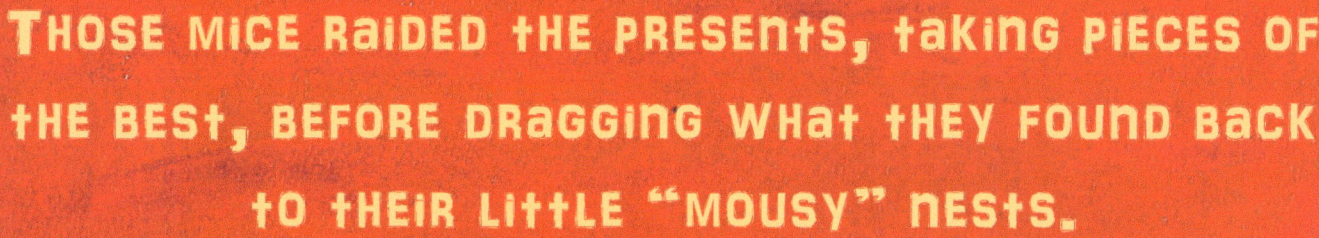

THOSE MICE RAIDED THE PRESENTS, TAKING PIECES OF THE BEST, BEFORE DRAGGING WHAT THEY FOUND BACK TO THEIR LITTLE "MOUSY" NESTS.

HOME SWEET NEST

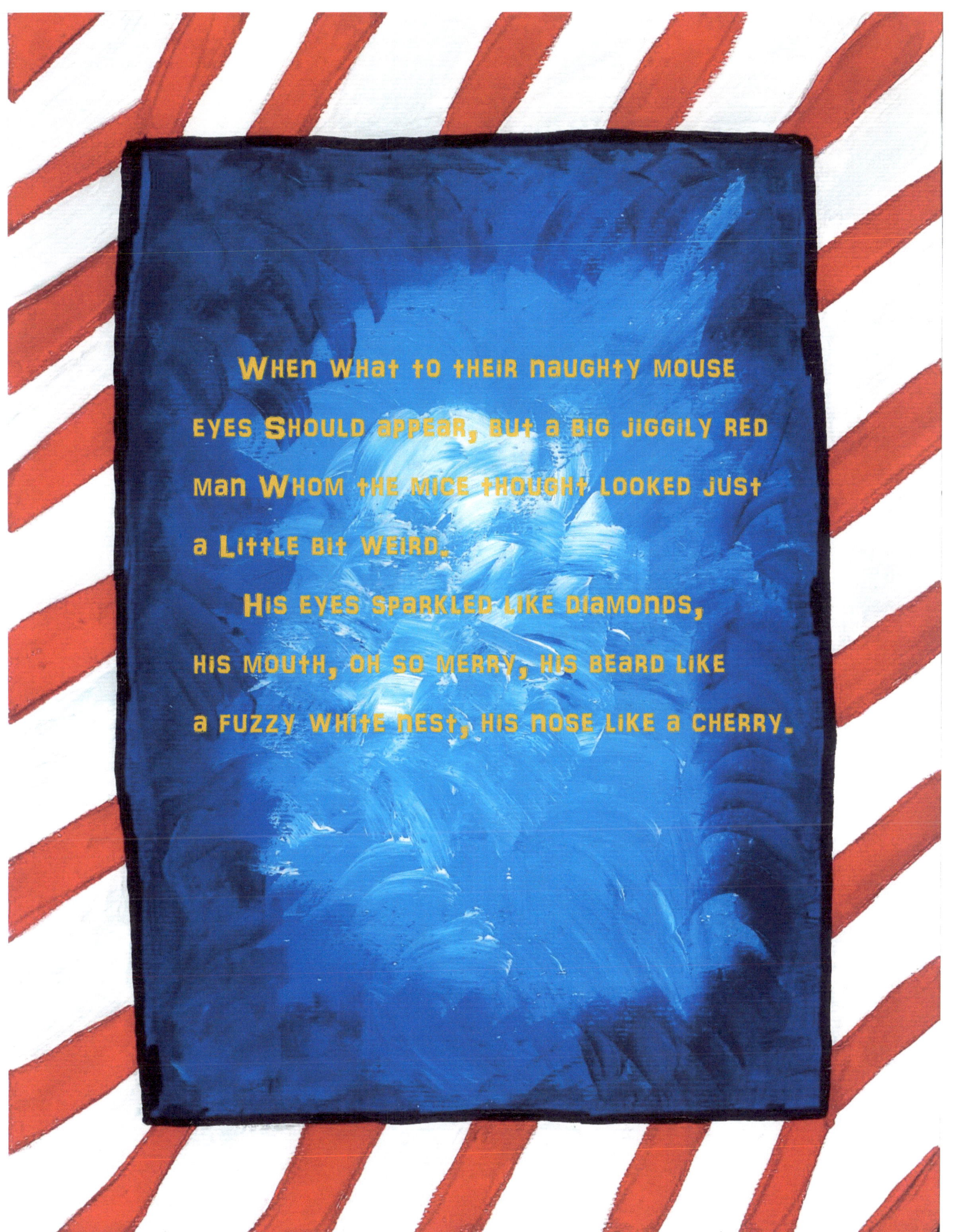

When what to their naughty mouse eyes should appear, but a big jiggily red man whom the mice thought looked just a little bit weird.

His eyes sparkled like diamonds, his mouth, oh so merry, his beard like a fuzzy white nest, his nose like a cherry.

"So, who was this strange man that was all dressed up in red? "

This was the question that caused each furry mouse to scratch his or her fuzzy head.

"I am Santa Clause" said the stranger with a chuckle in his voice, "I bring Christmas cheer to all of the good girls and boys.

You mice have been naughty this year it is true. Now I want this mess cleaned up by every one of you!"

But the mice simply stood there wondering what gave Santa the right to ruin their fun on that cold Christmas Eve night?

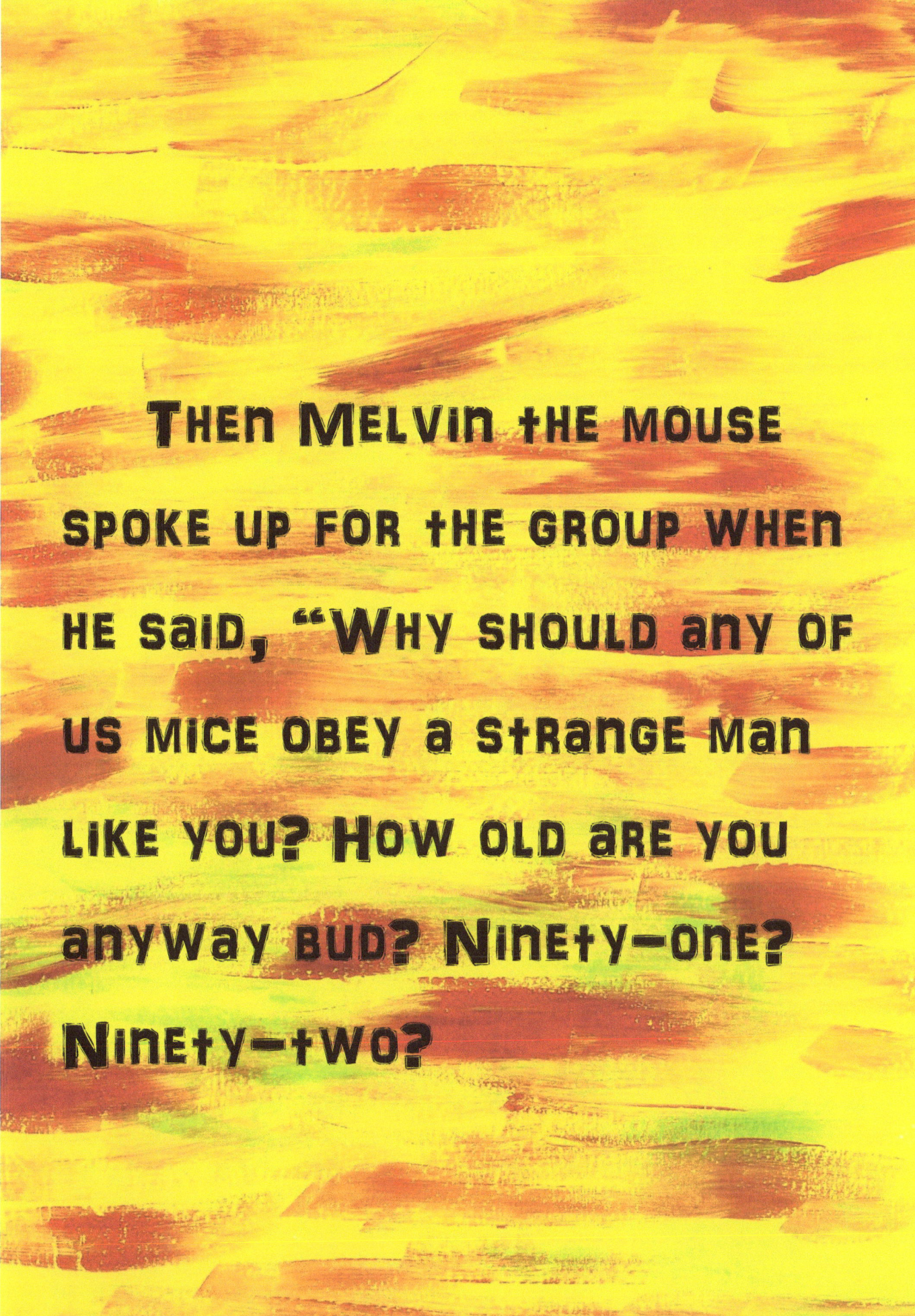

Then Melvin the mouse spoke up for the group when he said, "Why should any of us mice obey a strange man like you? How old are you anyway bud? Ninety-one? Ninety-two?

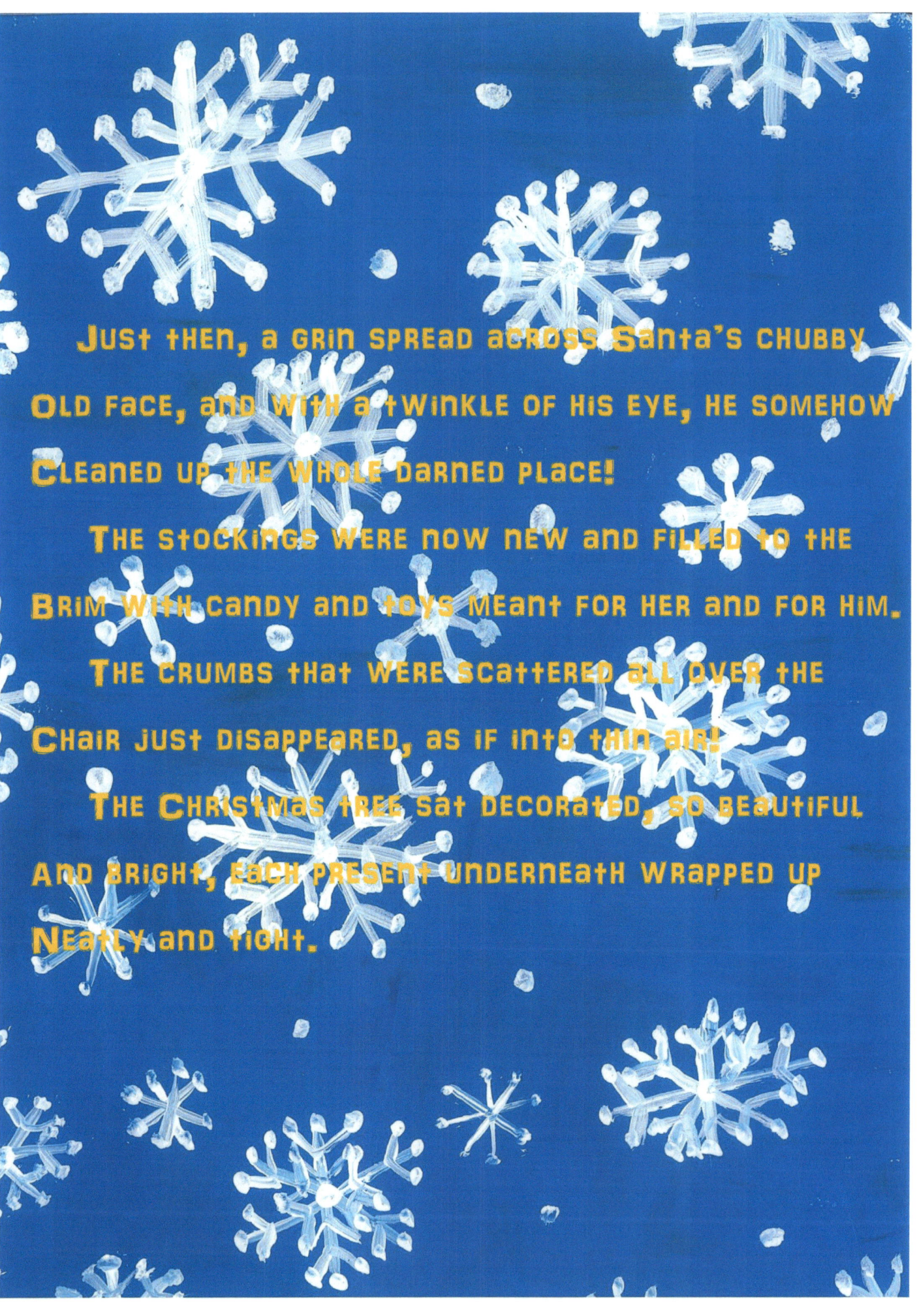

Just then, a grin spread across Santa's chubby old face, and with a twinkle of his eye, he somehow cleaned up the whole darned place!

The stockings were now new and filled to the brim with candy and toys meant for her and for him.

The crumbs that were scattered all over the chair just disappeared, as if into thin air!

The Christmas tree sat decorated, so beautiful and bright, each present underneath wrapped up neatly and tight.

THOSE MICE LOOKED AROUND AT THE NEWLY CLEANED HOUSE, NONE OF THEM VERY HAPPY AND SOME EVEN STARTED TO POUT! THEN MELVIN THE MOUSE SPOKE UP WITH A GRIN AS HE SHOUTED, "DON'T WORRY MY FRIENDS, WE WILL JUST START OVER AGAIN!"

WELL, it DIDN'T TAKE LONG
FOR THOSE MICE TO GET RIGHT
BACK TO THEIR MISCHIEVOUS
ACTS, MAKING MESSES
RIGHT IN FRONT OF SANTA
WHILE LAUGHING AND
SLAPPING EACH OTHER
ON FURRY, MOUSY
BACKS.

Again, Santa asked those mice to stop their naughty ways and to become good mice again for the rest of their little mousy days.

But the mice just ignored him as they made messes on the floor and if that weren't enough, Melvin even tried to show Santa to the door!

Santa calmly stood there watching those naughty little mice before starting to chuckle to himself as once again a twinkle came into his eye...

All at once, those mice started Growing larger, they lost their fur And tails, little mouse feet were soon Replaced with pointy shoes complete with Shiny jingly bells!

Little men stared back at them with round
faces all aglow, how Santa had replaced their
fuzzy mouse fur, they really didn't know.

Santa started to speak again
with his jolly old voice,
"You see little mice, since
you wouldn't obey, a
lifetime of toy making
is the price you will pay.
There is plenty of room for
all of you up North in my
shop, but your mess making
and mischievous ways will
just have to stop!"

FROM that day FORWARD those MiCE BECAME SOME OF Santa's BEST ELVES. THEY HELPED Santa MAKE PRESENTS And stocked toys on His SHELVES.

THEY ARE COMPLETELY HAPPY EATING HUNDREDS OF
COOKIES EACH DAY AS THEY SAND, PAINT, AND HAMMER AWAY.

THERE IS a LESSON to BE LEARNED FROM this ODDLY MOUSY taLE, and if YOU CHOOSE to HEED THESE WORDS YOU WILL LIKELY NEVER FaiL.

"DO WHAT YOU'RE TOLD AND GET it DONE, OR YOU MAY NOT LIKE WHAT YOU BECOME!"

Heather Gilbert is the author of "The Mice Before Christmas", as well as; "Skyler the Pirate", "Toys For Sale", and "A Slightly Odd Alphabet Book". She lives in Southern Utah With her Four Children, Husband, and dog Mia.

www.ingramcontent.com/pod-product-compliance
Lightning Source LLC
Chambersburg PA
CBHW041620120626
46551CB00003B/519